DANGEROUS SPACE

FIVE TALES OF WILD SPACE ADVENTURE

STEFON MEARS

Also by Stefon Mears

The Rise of Magic Series
Magician's Choice
Sleight of Mind
Lunar Alchemy
Three Fae Monte
The Sphinx Principle
Double Backed Magic

Cavan Oltblood Series
Half a Wizard
The Ice Dagger
Spells of Undeath

Power City Tales
Not Quite Bulletproof
No Money in Heroism

Standalones
Between the Cracks
Sects and the City
Prince of a Thousand Worlds
Devil's Night
Portal-Land, Oregon
Stealing from Pirates
Fade to Gold
With a Broken Sword
Twice Against the Dragon
The House on Cedar Street
Sudden Death
On the Edge of Faerie

Short Story Collections
Spell Slingers
Twisted Timelines
Longhairs and Short Tales: A Collection of Cat Stories
Confronting Legends (Spells & Swords Vol. 1)
The Patreon Collection, Vol. 1-7 (Vol. 8, coming soon)

Nonfiction
The 30-Day Novel and Beyond!

Spells for Hire Series
Devil's Shoestring
Zombie Powder
Spirit Trap
Dragon's Blood

The Telepath Trilogy
Surviving Telepathy
Immoral Telepathy
Targeting Telepathy

Edge of Humanity Series
Caught Between Monsters
Hunting Monsters

Published by Thousand Faces Publishing, Portland, Oregon

http://1kfaces.com

ISBN:

DANGEROUS SPACE

CONTENTS

THE FINAL SURVEY OF
ANDREI KREUTZMANN

Pilot's seats shouldn't be as comfortable as the second-hand, broken-in couch I had in flight school. But the whole cabin of my little pyramid of a ship is no more than twelve meters square. There's no room for a bunk. So I'm drowsing for the third time today when the sensor alert starts its incessant beeping, like a yappy dog who wakes you up at three hundred hours to go for a walk, and you know you have to get up or he'll piss all over your shoes again.

Yeah, sometimes I'm glad Sheila and her dog are gone.

At least with the survey ship I get to do what I never got to with the little yapper: I slap the big red button on the console hard enough to feel a satisfying sting reverberate through my fingers and wrist that lasts for seconds.

"I'm awake, I'm awake," I grumble through a yawn. "What have we got?"

"Viable asteroid," says the *Drever* in the pleasant tones of holovid star Monica Sellers, like every report is a seduction. Weird to hear her voice talking about mineral readouts, but the Monica Sellers dreams I've been having every night while I go through this asteroid field near Sirius are worth a little weirdness. "Twenty-five point eight three three million tons of iron ore, purity sixty-two point nine nine three percent. Three point six seven seven million tons of ice, purity ninety-nine point nine nine eight percent..."

The *Drever* continues its breathy readout, but I wonder if it might be off this time. What are the chances of water that pure frozen on an asteroid with iron?

I swing my feet down off of the console and my boots clang on the metal deck. I lean forward on the console, smooth as I imagine Monica Seller's skin must be, but not as yielding. About as unblemished, though. I call it a console, but it has only three buttons, all big and candy-like: cherry red for 'acknowledge,' midnight blue for 'countermand,' and off in one corner, a medical white button with its purpose labelled in black block letters: EMERGENCY. Anything else you want, you have to talk to the ship for.

"Hold up," I say, interrupting the *Drever's* recitation of useful minerals at molybdenum. "Back to the ice. Prove it. Give me a taste."

The *Drever's* sensors feed it the data, and its holoprojector manifests the image of a chunk of ice in the air above the console. The *Drever's* holo is limited to the area above the console, but if that ice pans out I'll be able to afford a real ship, with an actual bunk so I don't need so comfortable a pilot's seat, and a galley that doesn't glitch its protein combinations and make every meal smell like lasagna with extra sausage.

I feel my heart rate kick up a notch, pulse points squeezing a little harder in my elbows and wrists as I stick out my tongue and flick it through the hologram: the taste is pure mountain lake after a snow. It tastes like money.

I'm going to be rich.

"Lock down the data, and triple-stamp the date, time and location, record safety protocol alpha, then--"

"Incoming transmission."

"Take a message. We have work to do." While I have the *Drever* repeat the scan for increased precision, I'll need to sift through the data. Ice is the big discovery, but if the iron is that impure, there may be a secondary find in the impurities...

"Message response overridden, priority code three eight three seven."

Cold sweeps over me like I'd dunked my whole face in the ice holo. That's my military override code. I'm three years into my five-year post service reserve period, and I haven't heard a peep on an official channel since I took off my fatigues. Figures that just as something really good is happening I get the call.

"Grace period expiring," says the *Drever*. "Opening channel."

"Squad Leader Andrei Kreutzmann?"

No image yet, but the voice sounds as young as I was the first time I sat in a pilot's seat. "No squad to lead these days, but the rest is right."

"Please confirm your service number?"

"Red alpha three eight seven eight." The words snap out before I think about them. Guess that says something about how many times I've answered that request.

"Transferring you to Marshal Adler." The holo forms the spinning cube I've seen a thousand times, once face the Imperial logo of House Kuhn, the other five the symbols of the branches of the imperial military. Then the holo forms the dark cragged face I'd reported to since she was only a captain, Wilhelmina Adler. My hand salutes before I realize I've done it.

"Kreutzmann," she says as she returns the salute. "I'm officially restoring you to active duty under general order thirty-two, subsection twenty-eight eff."

Wait. Isn't that urgent need in a combat zone? Is that why I'm talking to a marshal instead of an adjutant? "Um, Marshal? I don't exactly have a fighter out here."

"You have a Duncan-Kessler Two Eight Six Deep Space Scout. As of right now it's commandeered."

"But I have a find--"

"So log it. We're not in touch with home so we can't submit it for you." She gives me a glare, as though daring me to argue, but her glares have always clamped my lips shut and made my back stretch straighter, which would feel fine if I were standing at attention, but sitting in my too-comfortable seat feels more than a little ridiculous. Once she decides I'm done debating, she continues, "I need you to confirm conditions at our escape hatch, Coriolanus Three."

"I did the survey work on that one." It paid for the computer upgrade on the *Drever* and that house on Io that Sheila claimed was so important for us, then decided was too big when I had to be gone for weeks at a time. "I can tell you all about it right now--"

"If I want old data I'll ask for it. You will go to Coriolanus Three and get me a complete report of *current* conditions."

"Yes, Sir!" Three years out and I still snap to attention when I hear that tone, that little extra force all commanders seem to be able to put behind their words when they want to. Makes me want to kick myself when I realize I'm standing alone on my own ship.

Then the spinning cube is back, and the *Drever* says, "Incoming mission data."

At least the voice module makes those words sound sexy. Takes some of the sting out of delaying my claim on this asteroid. I bring the orders up on the holo, but they don't look any more complicated than Adler made it sound: jump to Coriolanus Three, take enough readings to confirm its usefulness for emergency repairs and re-supply, report in, then I'm my own man again.

Correction, I think with a slow smile. *Then I'm a* rich *man.*

THE JUMP TO CORIOLANUS THREE TAKES ABOUT FOUR HOURS from the ass-end of space where I had been going through that asteroid field. Too long for a nap, but not enough time for real sleep. So, when the arrival alert buzzes I wake up dull, hot through the face, and feeling like someone filled my limbs and torso with iron ore (purity sixty-two point nine nine three percent). My feet slide off the console and slap down hard against the deck, my neck kinks, I would swear I smell salami (though it may just be my breath) and I just don't fit right in my body. It takes me three tries to say, "Status?"

"Ten minutes from touchdown on Coriolanus Three," says the *Drever*, and Monica Sellers' sweet tones make me want to settle back into the seat and just let the ship talk to me. "I have us in tidally locked orbit around its moon."

"What?" I look out the front viewport and see the gray and blue surface of the moon. I'm starting to feel like my muscles are in the right place, so I sit up and rub my neck, but I still don't see anything but the moon and the deeper blue edges of C3, like a rim around the moon. "Why? We can't survey from this position?"

"Security protocol delta."

The cobwebs are finally starting to clear in my head, but I waste a moment scrunching up my face and trying to remember the protocols I established back when I first got the *Drever*. Then it hits me, clenching my stomach and giving me an urgent need to hit the head. "Enemy ships? How many?"

"Unknown." The holo forms an image of high orbit over C3, blurred as the sensors adjusted from the jump, but with enough bogeys to imply an attack force. "Estimated three carriers, four line ships, two dozen support and over hundred fighters."

"How reliable is that estimate?"

"Sixty percent certainty."

For the first time, I regret installing the Monica Sellers voice module. Her voice should be saying sexy things and telling me I'm getting rich, not telling me about warships.

"If I ask you to open a channel to the fleet, what are the chances of one of these ships picking up the signal?"

"Impossible to establish with certainty, estimated ninety-two percent."

I start to shake my head, but the kink in my neck complains. I wander three whole steps over to the production unit that serves as a galley for an anti-inflammatory and a little water. Then I fold down the head and take care of my enemy-sighted jitters.

I sit there longer than I have to though, just thinking. I could spin out, just jump back to that asteroid field and report that C3 was a no-go. But that isn't my call to make, it's Adler's. She didn't send me here to evaluate it as an escape hatch, she sent me for a status report. Which means she might be expecting trouble, maybe needs to know what she has to clear to use it as an escape hatch.

Then I realize I'm delaying because I don't want to face the truth: this call is above my pay grade. I've been making my own decisions for so long, I've forgotten what it means to serve. Adler sent me here for a full readout, and it doesn't matter if she's expecting trouble, wants trouble, or if C3 is the target now and not an escape hatch. She needs the data, which means everyone under her command is relying on me to get it, and the difference between a vague report and a precise report could be thousands, maybe millions of lives.

I flush, re-seal my pants, fold back the head, and run my hands through the chemical cleanser. It's time to go to work. First I have the ship run an update analysis on the moon, so this time in orbit isn't wasted. But when it finishes I lose my excuse to sit here in my comfy hiding place.

Coriolanus Three's moon is too small to have any atmosphere worth noticing, so I don't make a re-entry burn when I bring the *Drever* down low enough that a tiny speck of a ship like mine shouldn't be noticeable to their outfliers as I come around the horizon and start to get a look at what's out there. The viewport isn't much good for this, not at this distance, but once the moon's shadow is out of the way of my sensors I can get a holo-display of the layout. Turns out to be four carriers and six capital ships, but I can't get a good count of support craft and fighters from here. Current guess is about thirty and one-twenty, but I know that isn't good enough.

Worse, I don't know these designs. If this is the enemy, then it's one I haven't fought. But that could be, because I haven't been keeping up with politics since I left active duty. Still, I know they aren't us and I know they aren't allies, otherwise I wouldn't be here. But they could be pirates, or even some kind of neutral party, if someone managed to jump the imperial claim on this planet.

"Do we have any friend or foe data that matches these ships?"

"I'm sorry," says the *Drever*. "No friend or foe data modules have been installed. Would you like to request an upgrade at the next port?"

Of course not. I never thought I'd need them. So even if the mission profile they sent me includes them, I can't get to them. Realization closes my eyes, makes me sit back in my chair, which doesn't feel all that comfortable at the moment. If those are enemy ships, then I'm in a live-fire zone on Imperial business, with no markings on my ship or uniform on my back.

Right now I'm not just a scout. I'm a spy. Scouts get shot down, but when they catch spies...

I want to leave. I want to turn tail and run, jump somewhere, anywhere. The asteroid field. Io. Earth. Maybe I can find Sheila, beg her to give me another chance, log that asteroid find in her name so she knows I'll stop running to deep space every time we fight.

I can bring solid data with me. I can get a detailed readout on the planet from here. Even the initial scan shows it's still habitable, arable, and if the atmospheric readings are right, still basically untouched. Even its mineral deposits...

Wait.

Coriolanus Three *is* untouched. Completely. That gives my mind a problem that stops the spiral of panic. There's no reason a perfectly good planet should sit uncolonized for two whole years since I logged the find. I start to wonder how that could be, but the answer is obvious: either it's disputed territory or the military held it in check, say, as an escape hatch. Adler probably expects this to be a routine scan, which explains why she sent someone like me, unmarked and halfway back to civilian life. Why waste a military scout when a surveyor can do the job?

But it's not my place to speculate motive. And a quick word in that sexy voice tells me the early scans are confirmed. I could leave with solid data on the planet, rough data on those ships and my hide intact... But the words of an old fleet saying flit through my head:

Half a report is worse than none.

I have to go in closer. I have to know what those ships are.

"Show me their formation."

The holo brings up marker images of Coriolanus Three and its moon, for reference, then pans in to show the foreign ships arrayed in a spiral diamond formation, with one capitol ship at the vertex, then spreading half-spheres of fighters and support craft surrounding the other capital ships, and the carriers spread out in the back rank.

"You're not including the outfliers. Who's watching their perimeter?"

"No movement detected outside of formation."

The Quartati then. They don't use outfliers when they aren't expecting trouble. Enemy, then, unless there's been some incredible peace treaty in the last week. Probably preparing to jump...

Or waiting for someone to jump to them...

This is bad. I try to crack my neck to relieve the kink, but it refuses to cooperate. "Wait, those ships look plenty spread out to me. Why can't you get a count?"

"Unable to comply."

"What?" The *Drever* starts to repeat the only words that actually sound like something Monica Sellers might say to me, but I cut it off. "You can get me ore purity to the thousandths of a percent, but you can't count ships?"

"No military grade scanners have been installed. Would you like to request clearance for an upgrade at the next port?"

"Never mind." Of course. Limitations of civilian design: no weapons, no energy shields, and scanners that slide off of energy shields. If it weren't for the radiation grade sensors required for survey work I wouldn't have as much data as I do. "How close would we have to get?"

"We would have to close within eight thousand kilometers."

The effective weapon range of those capital ships might be up to ten thousand. Plus those fighters can all outfly me. If I get close enough to get a proper read, I'll never make it back out.

I slap myself to distract the building panic. I don't have to fly down their gullet. The whole formation is no more than a thousand klicks long.

"Prepare a transmission, military channel, top priority we can manage. Assemble all data we're getting from Coriolanus Three, its moon, and all those ships." I take a deep breath. "I want it prepped and its transmission assigned to the emergency button."

"Manufacturer protocol one requires--"

"Button override confirmation, Zeta Alpha Alpha Six Six."

"Password."

"Sheila."

"Working." I try to rub the kink out of my neck while I wait, to distract myself from the flutter in my stomach and the ache in my bowels and bladder that want me to hit the head again, even though I can't possible have anything left to get rid of. Finally Monica Sellers' voice says, "Shall I add information about asteroid two one two seven?"

"No," I start to say, but guilt heats under my collar. I can't let this find go just because I might not live to claim it. "Name stamp it with my name and Sheila Barksdale, then add the data to the transmission."

"Transmission ready."

"Keep recording, and add all new data to the transmission. If we're going to do this, we need to give them everything we can."

"Acknowledged."

"Also, set up a jump back to Earth, trigger set to the acknowledge button."

"Jump ready."

I step over to the hatch and grab my vacc suit, just in case. While I'm busy tucking in and setting it up so I can seal the vacc suit with a slap of one hand, the *Drever* takes us back around the lunar surface to the position tidally locked from the enemy fleet. Then I'm back strapped into my chair, and it's straight out for a thousand klicks, just to make sure I'm clear of their sensor range.

"Bring us back down toward the planet, down near the equator, along a nice arc away from those bad ships." As we get down toward the exosphere, I say, my voice quiet and a little sing-song, like I'm soothing an animal, "That's it, now skim the exosphere. Don't cross it. We leave a hint of burn those bad people will see us. Just ride it nice and close and take us toward the bad guys."

I can see the carriers now, tiny specks getting ever larger as the *Drever* moves to a point almost underneath them.

"Now," – I close my eyes for one more deep breath – "let's do a fly-by."

"Unable to comply. Manufacturer safety protocol three mandates that civilian ships cannot approach ships of--"

I slam my hand on the midnight blue countermand button.

"Ship, you take us closer."

"Unable to comply."

"Override! Personal passcode 'kill that damned dog.'"

"Unable to override manufacturer's safety pro--"

I slam the countermand button again. It doesn't help, but it does stop the reply.

"Fine. Give me the rudder."

"The manufacturer's warranty does not cover--"

"I said 'give me the rudder!'"

The holo display creates a joystick in slick black, with buttons on the front for forward acceleration and forward breaks. I take a control stick for the first time since I left my days as a combat pilot behind, and start the *Drever* forward, using just enough engine power to overcome C3's gravity.

Muscle memory tells me the response is sluggish. Training tells me the action is stupid. Even an academy plebe knows better than to fly an unfamiliar ship into a combat zone. And under manual control, the *Drever* is an unfamiliar ship.

"Distance to the closest carrier?"

"Nine thousand kilometers."

"So we're two thousand kilometers from being able to scan the whole formation?"

"Correct."

"Distance to the safe jump point?"

"Estimated safe jump distance, six thousand kilometers."

"Well, dead from enemy fire is no better than dead from a bad jump. Here we go!"

I trigger the engines as hard as I can. Acceleration sinks me into my chair – comfortable again – as the *Drever* burns up to full speed. Immediately I see two fighters break formation and move to intercept.

Fifteen hundred kilometers to full scan.

The first shots come from those fighters, plasma pulses missing wide by a fair margin. Establishing range, most likely. Still, I get that itch along my skin that comes from enemy fire, and my balls are clenching like they want back into my body. My back, stomach and shoulders are tight like it's my first dogfight all over again. I start the *Drever* spinning, hoping to diminish their chances of a good lock.

One thousand meters to full scan.

My wrist begs me to sweep back and forth, jink and juke to avoid enemy fire, but the *Drever* doesn't have the speed for good evasive maneuvers while closing the distance as fast as possible. I stick to spinning, but vary the pattern.

It doesn't help.

Plasma shots rip across the hull, shaking the ship with a sound like bacon thrown into a hot pan. Hull's too thin. I can smell the char. Maybe it's not the ship that's shaking.

Maybe it's just me. I know it's not a coolant leak wetting my face and pants. But, eyes closed for a moment with prayer, I keep that accelerator down.

Five hundred meters to full scan.

Two more shots burn my tail and my left hand is sore from slapping the countermand button. I don't need more updates on the ship's damage. The hull is shaking so bad it's rattling my teeth. The charred metal smell fills my nose. My white-knuckled grip on the stick keeps the top speed I can get, but my wrist has overcome my reason and I'm throwing in whatever little jumps and slips I can coax the *Drever* to manage.

Two more shots rock my tail and I hear Monica Sellers' voice utter the two words every spacer fears most: "Hull breach."

I slap the seal on my vacc suit and feel it puff around me. The charred smell is gone now, but the transmitter link in my helmet keeps me in touch with the ship, which enables me to hear those three little words sent from heaven: "Full scan complete."

I slap the emergency button with my left hand while prying my right hand off the stick. If I read the display right, I manage to slap the jump button just as two more shots are incoming. The last thing I hear before the jump engine kicks in is, "Transmission complete."

I ARRIVE IN WHAT WOULD BE GEOSYNCHRONOUS ORBIT ABOVE the Earth, except I no longer have a ship. Just a bunch of floating debris around me – and too few to be all of them – where I sit still strapped into my pilot's chair, which yet remains bolted to part of the deck.

I guess the ship didn't survive the jump. Good thing I'm in my vacc suit.

I'm sorry to lose the *Drever*, but since Adler commandeered it, I'll make sure she pays me its full value it when she contacts me to tell me how many lives my actions today saved. And she will. She's a rough old warbird, but when she finds out what she threw me up against, she may even give me a medal. That would sure look good to Sheila when I track her down to tell her we're rich. Might even get her to take me back.

For now all I can do is trigger the emergency beeper in my vacc suit. I only have two hours of air, but this is Earth. If I read that flare right, one of the local patrol boats is already on its way to pick me up.

For now, at least my chair is comfortable.

MY DEAD FATHER'S SIGNAL

I found my father's boots orbiting Pluto.

I was out there on a routine news hunt. Ever since the discovery of Ymirite – the heavy metal isotope that all the experts said would one day revolutionize space travel – Pluto'd been a pretty happening place. Three space stations in orbit. Mining domes on the surface. Infighting among the local corporations. Infighting in the blossoming political structure. *Actual* fighting among drunken miners. Always some kind of news to find on Pluto.

Just the sort of place a reporter like me got to go on assignment every few months.

Back then I wasn't just Jason Neuhaus, I was *Jason Neuhaus*. Top field reporter for the Solar News Network. "The Galaxy's News Source." What a joke. Mind you, we humans did have eight settlements off of our home planet, but none of them were outside the heliosphere, so "galaxy" was a *wee* bit of an exaggeration. Especially since we'd already known about the Sarkaanan, a lizard-like space-faring race, for the better part of a decade.

Typical, really.

Anyway, I was out there in the SNN3, which was the first of the Cronkite-class vessels: half-ship, half-camera. Just me, of course. The network would never spring for a pilot, and the latest tiny drone cameras had finally made photography specialists a relic of history.

Just as well. Only room for one in the SNN3, and I loved flying that thing. Did most of my pilot training in those old shuttle-style ships – the kind that look like bloated airplanes – that still serve for economy class travel. And let me tell you, after dragging around in those behemoths, the SNN3 was pure joy. Swift and maneuverable as a flying disc. Modeled after old ideas of flying saucers, with cameras top and bottom, and a third on a track so it could be anywhere along the rim. Internal camera at the pilot's station too, for when SNN wanted to put their field reporter on camera.

Not a bubble-top ship, of course. The bubble-tops were no good inside an atmosphere, and an SNN ship had to be able to go anywhere. Heck, I once took the SNN3 into the seas of Neptune...

That's for another time though.

Cronkite-class ships had one room on the inside, and every inch of it was chromed glossy like the outside. Smelled glossy, too, until I'd been in it enough days to give it more of a bachelor aroma, like sweat socks and lasagna. The room was round like the outside and just tall enough that even I could stand up, and I stand just shy of two meters. No gravity, of course, but I was long used to floating everywhere and letting the magnets in my gray jumpsuit tack me to anything that mattered. That's just how we did things in those days.

The cabin had a pop-down bunk, pop-up head, and cabinet panels for everything from food to food preparation to storage.

And, of course, the pilot's station, console, view screen, and a fixed, padded chair with adjustable head and arm rests.

Everything ran through that station. The exterior cameras fed the same master view screen as the sensors. In fact, every iota of information the ship gathered or the recording equipment required routed through the same view screen, which could be compartmentalized as needed, of course.

The ship's recorders ran nonstop unless I hit the big red kill button on the right hand side of the pilot's station. As opposed to the big red button on the left side of the station, which was the emergency beacon.

Woe betide the journalist who got them confused.

Those were two of only five physical buttons on the pilot's console. The other three were at the front edge, just in front of the pilot's seat and determined which virtual controls showed up on the console: pilot, editor, or repair/diagnostic.

So I'd been at Pluto about two days, finishing up a story about the struggle against corruption in the burgeoning local government. Seems the corporations were trying to buy their way in, and the miners who were settling there wanted to govern themselves without interference from their employers.

I had that story finished and in the can, and truth to tell, it was just about time for me to head back. But I wanted to fit in another story while I was here at the ass-end of our little solar system.

I wanted to do a side story, human interest bit, about why anybody would want to live on Pluto. There had to be something beyond just work or frontier life. The only problem was that I had yet to find any other angle I could believe. And I was the guy who covered that doomsday cult who settled on Mercury.

Yeah, that one ended about how you'd expect.

Closest I could come so far was, "You won't believe the snow forts." I was ready to junk that, though, and try "Yeti Women of Pluto and the Men Who Love Them." If only I could find some shot I could pass off as a female yeti.

I was sitting at the station, going through my shots of the locals in their pseudofurs, when my proximity sensor started pinging. I brought up the view on the rotator camera, and there they were.

A pair of white spacesuit boots. Magnetic. Stuck together toe-to-heel, Velcro straps undone. Tiny little things.

Wouldn't make a sound when they bounced off my hull. But somehow they'd tripped the proximity sensor.

I had to swap over to pilot's controls to start riffling through serious information from the sensors – anything more than *oh shit notice this!* really – and then I only needed a few seconds to realize I was getting a transponder code. From a pair of boots.

And I recognized the code.

My dad, back when he was flying, used to scout for Earth. No, not in those archaic shuttles like they showed on the news. He flew the real military scout ships. The ones that looked like darts the color of gunmetal, and they flew faster and farther than anything else we'd developed.

I wasn't supposed to know that, of course. Same as I wasn't supposed to know that he disappeared on his last mission a decade ago. The official story was that he'd flown out to Pluto carrying cargo for the space station construction crews, and that after he'd dropped off his last load his ship malfunction and exploded.

But I knew a couple of other things I wasn't supposed to know. Like that Dad was actually going out beyond the heliosphere. That the coincidence of timing between Dad's disappearance and our discovery of the Sarkaanan spoke volumes about what had actually become of my father.

I also knew that Dad used to hide a comm in his spacesuit, in case he got stranded. He used to set it to broadcast an I.D. signal, just in case. And I knew that signal when I saw it on the view screen.

Faded. Weak, after all these years, and maybe never all that strong to begin with. I do know that if the boots hadn't been so close to my ship, I might never have picked up their transmission.

But I did. And I used the SNN3's cargo arm to grab those

boots. I couldn't bring them inside. Not in space. Cronkite-class ships weren't designed for it. The cargo arm would have brought the boots directly into the cabin, and that meant depressurizing. Risking my food supply, heck, all my supplies.

But now that I had the boots, I could put on my helmet. Go out through the emergency hatch sealed behind one of the cabinets. Risky, but less so.

Or I could just fly nice and slow to one of the space stations, dock, and get the boots that way. That made the most sense.

My comm pinged. Emergency frequency. As soon as I opened up the channel, a harsh voice said, "Attention SNN3, this is Pluto Patrol. Release the contraband immediately or face the consequences."

WHEN I WAS LEARNING TO FLY SPACE SHIPS, EVERY INSTRUCTOR emphasized over and over – always obey planetary patrols and naval commands. And they had a point. Space is no joke, and the only times most civilian pilots will get any kind of instructions from an official source there's a solid survival-based reason for compliance.

But my dad didn't raise obedient sons.

"Roger, Pluto Patrol," I said. "I'll be more than happy to release any contraband I come across. But until I actually *find* some, I'm going to have trouble complying."

As I spoke, I did what I should probably have done as soon as I had the boots in the grip of my cargo arm – put the cargo arm away. The arm was big enough that the little pair of boots would have no trouble fitting in its compartment when the arm folded up.

I hated doing it though. I wanted my dad's boots *now*. I wanted to look at them. Hold them. These were the first remains of his I'd been able to find, and, well, I didn't want to wait to get my hands on them.

I didn't see a choice though. I slapped the virtual button to put the arm away while I glanced at the sensor readout to find the Pluto Patrol ships.

Three blips, flying wedge formation. And they were between me and the space stations.

"Don't play games, SNN3," said the harsh voice. "Your sensors weren't the only ones picking up that signal. We don't know how you got here first, but this is Pluto space. You can't claim scavenger's rights."

Wait, they only just picked up the signal? Did the boots just start transmitting? Could Dad have planned far enough ahead to know I'd be using my reporter's credentials as my transponder code?

Of course! It's not like that would have changed. And he would have known the I.D. code. He must have set the comm to start transmitting when my signal came in range.

"Never said anything about scavenger's rights, Pluto Patrol. In fact..." I sighed, exaggerating the gesture as a show for the console camera. "Look, who am I dealing with?"

"This is Lieutenant Stewart, and you're five seconds away from a world of trouble, SNN3."

"Thank you, Lieutenant. I wanted to make sure SNN has your name right when they broadcast a report of this incident. Because if you got my transponder code, then you might recognize the name. Jason Neuhaus. Top field reporter. Ring a bell?"

I smiled when the lieutenant didn't reply immediately.

"Hold position, SNN3. Move so much as a klick from your current position and we will blast you out of the sky."

"Roger that," I said. But I had a problem. Either the boots were bigger than I thought, or their magnets were causing a problem. The cargo arm was still extended. I tapped the button to put it away, but the button flashed red.

I toggled the console over to repairs/diagnostic mode, and the readout confirmed what I'd already deduced. I couldn't put the cargo arm away until I did something about the boots.

So much for hopes of a quick getaway. The SNN3 might just have been fast enough to outfly the Pluto Patrol ships. Might even have been fast enough to outfly their rockets, if I got extremely lucky. But if I tried that kind of speed, the pressure on the cargo arm would snap it at one of the joints.

Better to turn the boots over than lose them that way.

"SNN3," said the harsh lieutenant, "you are instructed to accompany us to Space Station Alpha immediately, where you will hand over your contraband."

I wasn't sure why they chose Station Alpha, but if they wanted me to go there, I wanted to go elsewhere.

"Negative, Pluto Patrol," I said. "Guys, I'm late for an appointment in Dome Omega now. Why don't you just follow me down there and we can figure out what you think I have that's contraband. Because I say again, I have no contraband. To count as contraband, something would have to be illegal to possess or illegal to transport. And all I've done is grab some debris that was causing problems for my sensors."

"Release the debris," said the lieutenant. "We'll take care of it and you'll make your appointment."

"Negative," I said with a heavy sigh. "I don't have time to wait for you guys. Follow me down and we'll figure this out on the ground. I'll fly nice and slow, so you can't complain I'm trying to lose you."

Actually, I wanted to fly nice and slow to minimize the risk of losing the boots. Pluto didn't have much of an atmosphere this time of year, but any was more than I wanted to deal with.

Unfortunately, the Pluto Patrol didn't want to let me go even that far.

***

THE THREE SHIPS SURROUNDED ME BEFORE I'D GOTTEN MORE than a klick, and I got a good look at Pluto Patrol ships for the first time. They had cigar bodies that would have been completely useless in an atmosphere. Not a single wing or flap anywhere. They were black as space, with a series of green and red running lights the only way to tell which way they faced.

No way I could have outflown those things. Well, in an atmosphere I could have, but not here in space. No chance. They were sleek, with three rings of steering engines – one set fore, one set amidships and one set aft – that could make those ships corner like cats on shag carpeting, and I didn't doubt the thrusting power of their main engines.

They might not have had the fuel to chase me all the way to Mars, but they wouldn't have to.

And the Pluto Patrol did have rockets. Each ship had four, equidistant around the hull. All facing forward, which was something. If they fired while I was moving behind them, the rockets would have to take time and space to turn, and...

"This is your last warning, SNN3. Release your contraband."

"Galley," I called across the small cabin, "brew me double-strength coffee, stat."

I could smell it starting to brew as I formulated my lie.

"I've been trying to be nice about this, Pluto Patrol," I said. "But you're giving me no choice. With my life in danger, I'll have to invoke Free Press Right 116, guaranteed at the last Convocation. Everything in my ship records, including my medical information, and our current conversation is being transmitted along an SNN emergency frequency. If you destroy me now, you're doing so in a live, interplanetary broadcast. So, any last words before you fire?"

I did open a channel. And I did transmit tons of data, way more than they could hope to analyze quickly. The data was everything my cameras had recorded since I set out a week ago. Absolutely everything, even me sleeping and using the head.

But there was no one on the other end of that channel, much less any kind of live broadcast. That kind of thing had to be setup well in advance, and with the time delays inherent in long-range communication, they were usually a disaster.

Oh, and Free Press Right 116 said only that no local government shall inhibit the movement of registered journalism ships without due cause. And the definition of "due cause" went on for more screens than I cared to count.

"You are in possession of items designated contraband by Pluto. We are—"

"What items?" The lieutenant wasn't the only one who could make his voice harsh. And I had years of reporting experience behind me.

"Boots that—"

"Boots are not an item on any list of controlled substances or restricted possessions filed by any Earth territory." I hadn't checked, but it sounded reasonable. They were boots, for crying out loud.

"Everything involved in... Those boots..."

"Pluto has six events registered as historically important. Which do you claim these boots apply to?"

The moment the words were out of my mouth I could have kicked myself. How could I have given him an out? Too much time away from covering politics, I supposed.

"The construction of Space Station Alpha."

"How can you be certain that these boots were involved in the construction of Space Station Alpha?"

"Their transponder code."

"I have a different record of that transponder code. I have it as registered to one Markus Neuhaus, Earth Naval—"

"Stop!" said Lieutenant Stewart. "Mr. Neuhaus, may we speak off the record?"

"Not with those rockets pointed at me."

Two of the patrol vessels moved off, and the third flipped one hundred eighty degrees in place, as though nothing could have been simpler.

I definitely could not have outflown these guys.

"This is the best I can give you," said the lieutenant. "Along with my personal guarantee not to fire on you if you don't try to fly off."

That was as good as I'd get. But it meant I had to do something I didn't want to do, because I knew they'd be able to tell if I hadn't. I didn't know for certain that they could tell, but their sensors were good enough to pick up the transmission from those boots at a vastly greater distance than mine had.

I slapped the stop-recording button.

"Thank you," said the lieutenant, and now he opened a

video link so I could see the man. Had to be pushing sixty, and his wrinkles were pushing it even harder. He had tanned skin, fine white hair, and brown eyes that told me clearly he wouldn't hesitate to fire if he had to.

"Mr. Neuhaus," he said, "I don't know what the big deal is with those boots, but I do know that their transponder code has been registered with the Pluto Patrol as Earth Ultra Secret. So they're a part of something bigger than either of us, and if you run a story about them you're going to run us all into about ten light years of hell."

"These boots belonged to my father. I want to take them home to—"

"Your *father*?" He looked even more incredulous than he sounded. "Come on. Just because you're both named Neuhaus doesn't mean I'm going to believe—"

I told him. I told him what my dad used to do, and I told him about the code. I even told him how my dad must have had those boots set to transmit when they picked up my reporter's I.D. number used as a transponder code.

"You could be shot for knowing those things."

"So could you," I said. "Now."

"Maybe." The lieutenant nodded back and forth. "But you definitely could. And when that story airs—"

"What story?"

I smiled as the realization spread over his face. My heart was pounding though, and a trickle of sweat beaded up between my shoulder blades. If I'd read this guy wrong, I was about to die.

"I always heard reporters are crazier than fighter pilots. Now I think I believe it."

"I don't want to run a story about the boots, lieutenant," I said, putting as much honesty into my eyes as I could manage. "I just want to take them home to my mother. A last token from her lost husband."

"I don't—"

"I even found them here in orbit around Pluto. Fits the official story of his ship blowing up after delivering his final load to the station construction crews."

"All right," he said. "Then let me get them for you."

At that point, there was no way I could say no. I wanted to. I wanted the patrol ships to fly away and let me go out the hatch for the boots myself.

Not that I was in such a hurry to go outside. Any kind of spacewalk is always a risk, and without anyone here to rescue me if something went wrong, even a quick jaunt to the cargo arm was risky. But I didn't want the lieutenant in my ship either.

But he had rockets, and I was about out of bluffs, so I didn't see any way I could get out of this.

I watched the lieutenant on the view screens, recording every second in case he betrayed me. True, I didn't want to go public about my father and the boots, but if he betrayed me I'd blow the lid off everything without a second thought or a moment of regret.

So I watched as Lieutenant Stewart came out into the black. His spacesuit was his dark blue uniform, with gray spherical patches to represent Pluto. He had a helmet on. The back matched his uniform, and it had a bubble plate in front.

His suit had wrist jets he used for a quick, controlled crossing from his ship to mine, bringing him directly to the cargo arm and the boots. I thought about not pushing the release button, but it didn't matter. He thumbed the manual release on the arm like he did it every day.

I had my hands on the pilot's controls then. If he made a single move back toward his ship, I'd ram him with mine. Yeah, his crew might kill me, but they wouldn't be able to save him.

That didn't matter either. He came right to the emergency hatch, and opened it when I tapped the release-to-manual virtual button. While I waited I prepped two space cups of coffee, pinch-able containers that used a liquid's cohesion to control how much came to the lip to drink.

Seconds later the hatch was closed and sealed, and he was stepping through a cabinet door and into my cabin. He stood about a quarter-meter shorter than me, but he was broader through the chest and shoulders. Looked like the kind of guy who started his day with a couple of hundred pushups.

And he had his right wrist jet trained on me like a gun, without a drop of mercy in those brown eyes, visible through his helmet.

"Whoa, now," I said, right hand coming up in surrender, but my left hand hovering over the transmit button. I didn't have any guns on the ship at all, much less at hand, but I did have a whole lot of data I could send that would make for one hell of a post-mortem story. "We're being friendly here, remember?"

"Take your hand away from the console," he said, and his voice almost metallic through his helmet.

"Lower the jet." My heart was pounding so fast now I could feel my pulse in my wrists, my fingers, my thighs. I was breathing so fast though my nose I could feel snot working its way down.

Lieutenant Stewart tossed the boots at my feet, where their magnets clung to the deck. Then he lowered the jet.

I eased my hand away from the button, but not too far. After all, he only needed to lift his arm and I'd be in a bad position again. Certainly my pulse didn't slow any.

"Let's be clear," he said. "I can't let you leave. Not with those boots and everything you've recorded. To be honest, I should probably have blasted you out of the sky the moment you tried to argue about contraband. But believe it or not, most of us in the military don't *like* to kill. We only do it when the job demands it."

"You can't keep me here." Not alive, anyway, and it was all I could do not to soil myself at the thought of dying out here, my death a lie like my father's.

"So this is what's going to happen," said the lieutenant. "You're going to erase every bit of data on this ship. All of it. Everything recorded, noted, or written up from the time you left wherever you came from."

"What about my report on—"

"Everything. And I'm going to check your work to make sure you do it."

"And if I agree?"

"If you agree you get to leave with your life and those boots. You just won't have any evidence of where you found them or how. Or your encounter with me and my men. Or—"

"Anything that could be remotely provable to anyone who'd care," I said. I didn't want to ask the next question, but I couldn't stop it. "And if I refuse?"

He raised the jet again. "Then I have to do a duty I really don't want to do."

I looked down at my dad's boots.

"All right," I said. "It's a deal."

I GOT FIRED, OF COURSE. GOING ALL THE WAY TO PLUTO AND coming back not just without a story, but without any data anyone else could use to generate a story. And without even a good explanation of what why.

Thinking back on it, I'm lucky they didn't sue me.

Anyway, I had to listen to three levels of bosses rake me over the coals before I was fired, and a loophole in my contract let them axe me without a severance package or anything, since they could claim misappropriation of resources.

I didn't care. They couldn't take away my pilot's license, so I knew I'd always have work. And I had something even more important, tucked away in my khaki canvas backpack. My dad's boots.

I caught a shuttle back to Earth, and from there to a little house in the high desert just outside of Tempe, Arizona. Since the eco-saving laws of the last century, Tempe'd become a nice place to live again. If you liked desert heat, and my mom did. Fortunately when I went there it was late fall, and the heat only dried the air made me aware of my skin, instead of drenching me in sweat and beating down on me like the time I visited in August.

I was, at least, smart enough to wear light, pale fabrics for my shirt and shorts, and sandals were practically an Arizona uniform.

Mom had a little one story ranch home done in faux-adobe, with a red, Mediterranean tile roof and natural dun and sand colors for the house itself.

I found her on the front porch, sitting in the wooden rocking chair that had been handed down through her side of the family for close to three hundred years. She was wearing a light red dress and a broad-brimmed hat, and came to her feet the minute she saw me, smiling brighter than the Tempe sun.

She still looked too thin to me, and I'd never get used to seeing my mother with all those wrinkles, but that smile told me she was feeling good, and there was strength in her arms when she hugged me tight.

I made her sit down again. Little worry lines frowned above her eyes when I set down the backpack and pulled out Dad's boots.

Maybe Lieutenant Stewart could stop me from *reporting* the truth about my father and his boots, but he couldn't stop me from telling my mother.

And I did.

THE INCIDENT ON GAMMA 7

THEY SAY THE STARS ARE BEAUTIFUL. NOT JUST WHITE POINTS of light out there in the blackness of space, but colorful nebulas and more. Swirls of reds and greens and blues, broader across than our dinky little solar system.

Well, I don't care how beautiful they are. I'm not going back.

I like blue skies above me, thank you very much. The pale blue of a cold spring morning here in the Pacific Northwest. The rich royal blue of high summer. Our clouds in their thousand and one shades of gray, from the little just-passing-through wisps to the towering giants full of lightning and thunder and driving rain, all the way to the quiet ones, as thick and fluffy as the flakes of snow they stream down once a year or so.

Those snowfalls only look intimidating, like this morning. A steady fall of white outside my window, covering the live oaks and pines and ferns and roses in my acre of a backyard, even the treelike arbor vitae shrubs lining my property. It looks like a frozen wonderland out there, as beautiful and dangerous as space, and just as unfeeling when it takes a life.

But here in my kitchen I'm warm. I can enjoy the view out my bay windows surrounded by the rich warm tones of real wood for my floors and my dinette set. Safer here than I ever was on a ship, much less an alien world, even if I do still keep a laser pistol on me at all times. All times. Even now it's in the right-hand pocket of my comfy blue terrycloth bathrobe. Silenced, which is illegal here on Earth like it is on every other planet we like to pretend we control, but if they come for me today I don't want to disturb my neighbors.

Disturbed neighbors call police. Police check DNA. DNA points to real names. Records. Records that include details like AWOL and desertion. Then my own people will be after my hide too.

After all, the records may have the details but they conveniently leave off the circumstances. I know. I've seen mine.

But they haven't come for me yet. So I sit here, linger over the crumbs of my cinnamon coffeecake, and sip my rich, home-blend of coffee. Mostly Argentine, with some of the more expensive Venusian for kick, and some mocha beans because I deserve them, Goddamn it, no matter what anybody says.

Twenty years I gave the Terran Naval Special Forces. Twenty years running ops across a hundred worlds. Some we pretend to control, like Ceti Five. Others, plainly in the paws of the Ik-Choka Empire, those huge, sapient, talking raccoons with their love of scatterguns and a relationship with trees I don't pretend to understand.

Worse were my days on Sarkaanan planets of the Kwa-rekk Federation. Like upright komodo dragons, the Sarkaanan. I get the shivers just thinking about the last time I watched any of them eat.

Sometimes I was there to spy. More often I had to pull the trigger. Or worse. All in the name of keeping their war going. Keeping their eyes on each other and not on us.

The things I had to do. If I'd been caught. If anything had been proven. Either the Kwa-rekk or the Ik-Choka or both would have wiped our little ape-derived species out of existence.

We humans may have our small corner of the cosmos, but we don't have the numbers or the firepower to hold it, no matter what the politicians say.

The galaxy belongs to the Ik-Choka and the Kwa-rekk.

We can only hope they kill each other off in their fight for domination and leave us alone.

I'm forty-eight now. I've got my scars. Even modern medicine can't keep my knee from aching when it rains. But that ache tells me I'm still alive. Tells me that that Ik-Choka and Kwa-rekk haven't found out yet. Don't know what I did. Or at least, aren't sure enough to send a death squad to Earth after me.

One more morning, yet, to savor my coffee.

Two years ago

I wasn't calling myself Doug McTavish then. I was still Commander Jeffrey Teague, in charge of the hardest bunch of vaccers that the government wouldn't admit existed.

Unit Seventeen.

Yeah, Unit Seventeen was real. Probably still is. More real than the Bermuda Triangle or the Flying Dutchman or the dragon that some people still believe is in the Ganymede no-fly zone.

There's no dragon there, folks. It's just a place to practice black ops maneuvers. Spent plenty of time there myself.

I was recruited for Unit Seventeen by the great Dick Hobbes. He grabbed three of us who graduated special ops training by the skin of our teeth, to fill out the whole team of eight.

Hobbes didn't want the guys at the top of the class, the gifted ones who coasted through training. He wanted the ones like me, the ones who weren't big enough or strong enough – maybe even not smart enough – for the job, but who fought every step of the way to prove we could do it.

That was what Unit Seventeen needed more than

anything else. Willpower. We had to keep going no matter what. The stakes were too big for us to lose, so we had to be the type who'd do anything to succeed.

I recruited the same way, once I was in charge. Hired the ones like me, the ones who believed in Earth and fought from the marrow of our bones on out.

When we touched down on the Kwa-rekk world of Gamma Seven that morning, we were loaded for snake. All eight of us had survived at least ten drops together, and we moved like a single organism.

The mission was simple enough. Gamma Seven had an ammo dump for special weapons. A little one, tucked just outside of some civilian zone so the Ik-Choka wouldn't spot it. Slip in and blow up the dump. Make it look like the Ik-Choka hit the place. Civilian casualties were discouraged, but not heavily.

Yeah, I know, but that was the way the orders were always phrased. They were going to deny us if we got caught anyway, so I liked to think they were trying not to tie our hands. That they'd rather we kill a few innocents and escape than get caught and put our entire species at risk.

But the truth was probably that the muckety-mucks upstairs thought a few civilian casualties would help fuel the tensions between the snake heads and the raccoons.

Either way, I was proud to say that, on my watch, Unit Seventeen had killed no civilians. What good was the human race surviving if we didn't stand for anything?

All eight of us coasted down out of the orange sky that morning on pop gliders, dressed for the environment in our red-brown camo with breather masks. The snake heads seemed to like our atmosphere well enough, but their planets never sat well with human physiology. One of the eggheads tried to explain it once, but I stopped him at "wear your breathers, just in case."

But the gravity was close enough. And some of the continents were green, in parts. Not anywhere near us though. We got the red zone, as usual.

Our armor plates weren't thick enough for a barrage of scattergun shot, and they'd go down after two hits from a hard beam rifle or one from a laser, but they were light enough not to get in our way, and they were coated to protected us from the acids the Sarkaanan used in their projectiles.

We were armed with scattergun rifles, hard beam pistols, and two knives each.

We touched down ten klicks from the depot, on red dirt that reminded me of Mars in those few canals still outside the terraformed zones. Gritty and dark, and so dry just looking at it made me thirsty. Dunes all around us, and tan trees with thick, rough bark and no leaves. Through the breather the air smelled astringent, and over the hissing sounds of my own breath I could hear a thin wind too high up for me to feel.

Inside I had the good tightness in my guts. I was ready to rock and roll. To keep the eyes of the big galactic predators off the human race for a little while longer.

We popped in the gliders. They folded back into the shoulder plates of our armor. I said a quick prayer that the lab boys estimated the fuel right, so we could fly back to the rendezvous point and not have to hoof it, possibly under fire.

So far, every mission had supplied enough fuel. But I prayed anyway, because it was too late to do anything if they hadn't.

I slapped the dirt, and every one of us dropped and

rolled around in it. The topsoil was loose, and in short order our pretty-good camo was looking *very* good. Any one of us could drop in the dirt and become almost invisible, if we had to.

I surveyed everybody to make sure we were good, then slapped three fingers on my chest and smacked my palm. Go sign for the three team split. Yeah, we had local comms, but comms always run the risk of being intercepted. On a mission we stuck to gestures as much as possible.

Wu, Gomez and Alvarez started off for their free-fire zone, ready to cover the rest of us if things went bad. Johnson and Duke had the explosive, so they had the job of getting in and wiring it up.

I took Jameson and Aminu with me to hack the security and set up a false feed as well as hide our tracks.

Chief Jameson was my right hand. A lean, mean redhead. She'd lost her left eye on a mission, but she could still shoot with the best and throw a knife better than anyone I'd ever seen. Scruffy bastard Aminu couldn't shoot for shit, by our standards, but he could hack anything with a chip and was small enough and brown enough that he could vanish in almost any environment, even when he wasn't covered in local dirt.

Without a word, we started for the security outpost and our part of the job.

THE SECURITY OUTPOST WASN'T *TOO* NEAR THE DEPOT. CLOSE enough to keep an eye on it without looking like there was anything to keep an eye on. Half a klick, maybe. The building itself was like most Sarkaanan buildings away from their homeworld. Like a great coiled snake. This one only had three loops, and the coils were only three meters across. Only maybe twice as big as the depot. It was orange, though, color coded for their military.

Four guards on patrol, with those bell-ended rifles they carried. Never did find out what the official name for them was. In the Navy we all called them Martini-Smiths, after the martini-glass shape of the end. They looked funny, but they could launch an acid ball hundreds of meters with deadly accuracy.

But this was the sort of thing we did all the time. Business as usual, except that, looking back, I think I had a bad feeling about it. Maybe that's just hindsight though, some part of me knowing that something was wrong before it was.

All I know for sure is that we were nestled safe and sound in the groove between two of the red dirt dunes a few hundred meters out from the security outpost. I kept an eye on the outpost with my field scope, making sure Aminu's hacking hadn't drawn any attention. First sign of consternation through one of the panel windows, first sign of action from a guard, it would have been shoot first and find out what happened later.

Meanwhile Jameson kept her eye in two directions. She'd check on the depot, making sure she didn't see any odd activity. Including our own troops, because if she could see them, then we had to assume the Sarkaanan could too, which meant it was showtime.

But she also checked the perimeter. Made sure there were no surprises coming.

Unfortunately, the surprises came from Aminu.

"Teague," said Aminu, urgency in his harsh whisper.

I nodded to Jameson to take over my watch and dropped back next to Aminu, who had a hacking cube unfolded into six panels of data and readouts, all in reddish-brown to go with the camo.

He didn't wait for my question.

"You're sure we've got the right site?"

I gave him a grimace for my answer. He knew I was sure. He knew I'd checked all the details of this assignment, right down to the fuel in our poppers, six times each at every stage. It was my ritual, and it was a ritual I firmly believed kept me alive.

He called up a camera feed and pointed to it. Sarkaanan hatchlings moving around. Tended by a few adults. Maps and simple words on the walls...

"A school?" I said.

"I can't find any sign of weapons there. It looks like a school on the edge of a community."

"Are you sure you aren't--"

"I know my job." Aminu's turn to grimace. "I'm so deep inside their systems that if we weren't genetically incompatible at least two of them would be pregnant. Ain't no weapons there, Commander."

I reached for my comm to signal *abort*, but Jameson slapped my hand.

"No depot there, *chief*," I said. "I'm calling this off."

"We have to blow the site, *commander*. Stay on mission."

"Job was to blow a weapons depot."

"No, the job was to blow the *site*. A weapons dump would have been a plus, but--"

"Those are civilians, Jameson. Children."

"Why do you think they always warn us about civilian casualties, Teague?" No warmth at all in her blue eye. "We blow the site."

"She's right, Commander," said Aminu, mouth screwed up as though his words tasted worse than the air. "Orders specified the building and location. Contents were listed elsewhere."

I knew Jameson and Aminu as well as I knew anyone. When we were off-duty we were friends. Heck, after one especially risky mission, Jameson and I ... well, looking into her cold eye I knew that didn't matter.

The only thing that mattered was the mission. Just like they'd always known. Just like I'd taught them myself. Every mission saved human lives.

But at what cost?

I nodded and turned away. Checked my watch. Johnson and Duke needed two more minutes yet to place the explosives and set the timers.

A lot could happen in two minutes.

We had a mission, though. The Sarkaanan had to believe the Ik-Choka assaulted this place. Blew up a...

Well, looking back I'd like to think I made a deliberate, calculated act. I'd like to think that all my years of military training and experience came to the fore, and I realized that a *failed* Ik-Choka mission could send the same mission. After all, the Sarkaanan had to find the explosives at the location. Had to know what was planned.

That was good enough. Right?

I tell myself that there was that much logic and planning that went into what I did next.

I grabbed my scattergun and slammed against the side of the dune. I opened fire on the guards and the security outpost. Gun shaking in my hand, vibrating me all the way down to my knees and up to chatter my teeth.

Behind me Aminu was swearing. Working double-time. Jameson's hand was forced. She called the combat retreat and joined me.

When Wu, Gomez and Alvarez opened up too it was like

a lethal hailstorm in the red, dusty air. My own breaths panting, wet inside the breather, that smell still astringent in my nose. Too far away for the dried shrimp and ammonia smell of the Sarkaanan themselves, but I imagined it with each one that went down in a spray of thin red blood.

In the distance, an explosion *boomed*.

AMINU COVERED OUR TRACKS. I KNOW THAT MUCH. Officially no report ever mentioned human involvement with the incident on Gamma Seven. I did ... dig a bit. I had to. I had to know what happened.

Facts are hard to come by from a war zone. Politics always get in the way. Body counts, damage estimates, they go up and down depending on what those in power want the rest of us to believe.

The Ik-Choka got the blame all right. The war got hotter for a while, and no one suspected humans had ever set foot on Gamma Seven. Officially, anyway.

As far as I could tell, Johnson and Duke hit the trigger before all of the explosives were in place. Blew out a third of the building's bottom coil. Killed maybe twenty.

I tell myself that it could have been much, much worse. Probably hundreds of kids in there. Little snake heads, all hoping to grow up and live good snake head lives. That doesn't even count the teachers and any other adults.

Maybe that day, for the first time since I enlisted, I saved a few nonhuman lives instead of taking them.

I "didn't make it" back to the rendezvous. I claimed to have been spotted. Separated from the group. Gave them orders to bug out while I pursued on foot to kill the witness. That way the most they could get was one of us.

Yeah, Jameson tried to argue that leave-no-man-behind thing. I gave her an order. Maybe the look in *my* eye spooked *her* for a change.

Once they were gone, I made my own way off Gamma Seven. I took the better part of a year laying false trails, just in case. I'm rated to do hull repairs, which meant I could find work on pretty much any ship flying, especially the type that wouldn't ask questions, if I didn't.

And I didn't want to answer or ask questions.

Eventually, though, I made it back to Earth to hide in plain sight. I set myself up someplace nobody knew me. I was an Arizona boy, born and bred. The PNW was just about the last place anyone would think to look for me. I'd hide here among the rain and the tall trees and avoid space like the plague. Act like an air-breathing rockfoot instead of a hardened vaccer. New name, new ID, and officially, no one had any reason to look for me.

Except...

Except that the Navy has to have figured out that I made it off of Gamma Seven. Otherwise the Sarkaanan would have said something about my corpse by now. Though maybe politics kept it quiet. Some high-level deal, maybe.

Except that the Ik-Choka know they weren't there on Gamma Seven. And that means there's only one spacefaring race who could have done it and pointed the fingers at them. Which means it's only a matter of time until they put the pieces together. At which point, no doubt Earth will hand me over wrapped up with a bow.

Except that the Sarkaanan have to wonder why the Ik-Choka didn't follow up the "failed" op with a bombing run to destroy evidence of what *was* there so they could claim a righteous military strike instead of espionage against a civilian target.

No, I was living on borrowed time and I knew it. One of these mornings I'd look out the bay windows of my kitchen and see a death squad coming for me. Maybe Sarkaanan. Maybe Ik-Choka. Maybe human. Maybe even led by Jameson.

But I still had a laser pistol. I'd make them work for it. Yes, sir.

And until then, I'll watch the snow fall, and sip my coffee, and try to tell myself I did the right thing that day.

◊◊◊◊◊

ONLY SHEEPDOG ON
THE MOON

Cole Douglas finished his afternoon jog through the scrub grass of the foothills. Half-assed job they did of terraforming Ganymede back during the great Deuterium Rush thirty years ago. Even the sky never got more than pale blue, which Cole blamed for his heavy breathing after only ten miles. Thin air from the bad terraforming, not age starting to rear its ugly head. Air didn't even taste fresh from last night's rain. It had that cloying little tang like he was around mold.

Besides, Cole was only fifty, not an old man yet.

Hands on his hips he walked in circles. No good going back to the bar sucking air like he was. Couldn't let the locals think he'd gone soft. Never hear the end of it then. Not that any of them had a right to point fingers about going soft. They liked their safe isolation on an ignored moon well inside Earth-controlled space, but not one of them ever served in the forces that maintained that safety. Much less faced five wars over twenty-five years and retired a full captain like Cole.

But he didn't mind a little teasing. They valued their privacy like he did, so none of them ever asked stupid questions about his service. They knew him as the bartender, and that was the way Cole liked it.

An orange flash high in the sky drew Cole's attention. He shaded his eyes and tried to look closer, but it was gone. Looked like an atmospheric entry, but the color was wrong and it was nowhere near the right trajectory to come near the little landing field the locals laughingly called their spaceport. He couldn't even hear a hint of its engines, just the three-note trill of a nearby spar-owl.

Could be low on fuel, he thought. *Must be a first-timer.*

Cole made his way down from the scrub and across the pale dirt toward the converted shuttlecraft that served as his bar. From the outside it looked like a bright red egg standing sideways on crab's legs. Cole grabbed a sharp rock and gave another halfhearted scrape at the Richardson Aeronautics logo, still mostly legible on the side. Cole called his bar The Final Resting Place. The locals just called it Richard's.

Cole scrambled up one of the crab legs to the cockpit up front where the egg tapered. He punched in his lock code and the canopy popped open, letting him into his sanctum sanctorum. Cole had only needed the controls that handled lights, power and comfort for the shuttle, so he had torn out most of the others to make room for his bunk and the hull-metal service chests that stored his clothes, books, vids and mementos. But Cole did keep the transmitter functioning, a superstitious fear going back to his days as a green private when the platoon transmitter got hit and...

Cole shook his head. That was all behind him now. He stripped for a quick chemical shower and came out smelling like cheap aftershave, too much musk and too little character.

He dressed in the spacer standard flexcotton long-sleeved shirt and slacks, his bright blue and dull grey, respectively. He entered the kitchen and supply area, converted from the former passenger cabin. He ignored the lingering grease smell from last night's sausages and fakeeggs and threw some prefabs in the heater so any early customers would have at least something to chew on. He was running low on local beer. That Henderson better not be late with his drop tomorrow.

Cole flicked on the lights in the main bar – once the cargo bay – and checked the levels of the bottles behind the converted chunk of hull he'd salvaged from that wreck an hour south from the 'port. Those all looked good, so even a run on beer wouldn't leave him dry. By reflex he also checked his old service weapon, an FMA 387 Hard Beam Rifle, kept under the bar. He kept the weapon ready for duty, though he never needed it, unlike the chunk of ship antenna he used as a club.

All ready, he flipped the switch to open the cargo bay doors and crossed between the bolted down tables and collapsible chairs to kick down the emergency ladder. He never lowered the cargo ramp, and the locals never asked him to.

AN HOUR LATER, COLE WAS LAUGHING ALONG WITH A HANDFUL the locals about a tour ship that came through last summer. The crowd that night was all-human, as usual. Officially Earth Gov. got on well enough with most of its neighboring sapients, but none of them ever asked to settle in Earth-controlled space.

So the crowd was a typical spread of a dozen locals near the bar, and close to twenty travelers near the back, usually smugglers and the sort who liked the way Ganymede thumbed its nose at government. Even the local governor hated reporting in to Earth, and ignored the regulation to maintain a standing militia. Who needed a militia when Earth had a military that covered a fifth of the Milky Way?

Cole didn't like breaking regs, but it wasn't his call to make.

"Any of you see that entry today?" asked Cole, interrupting old Zed's wide-eyed depiction of a rich, confused tourist. "Way off north, like the pilot doesn't even know where to land."

That got a little laugh out of the locals, but the travelers all looked up. One of them, a gruff looking kid with a scar, even if he was barely old enough to buy Cole's drinks, said, "I saw it. Snake-head orange."

Two of the tables of travelers emptied, their occupants hustling down the ladder fast enough to get a smirk or two out of the locals.

"No way it's the Sarkaanans," said Zed. "There's a cease-fire."

The kid shrugged and went back to drinking, but the travelers all grumbled among themselves like they agreed and needed to adjust their plans. Cole did remember something about new Sarkaanan engines burning orange, but it had to have been a trick of the thin atmosphere. Earth did have a cease-fire with Sarkaan. On the other hand, no one who moved to Ganymede tried to stay on top of the news.

Cole decided it was probably nothing, and distracted everyone by making up a story about how the Sarkaanans were coming to buy jinda weed from the governor.

By the time Cole ran the last drunks out of the bar for the night, he couldn't get the orange flash out of his head. He closed up the cargo bay and did something he hadn't done in a year-and-a-half, Earth standard time: fired up his transmitter. A quick call to the base on Europa would assuage any lingering fears.

The transmitter was a simple voice-only model that had controls like 'power,' 'volume' and 'frequency.' Little to go wrong and little to break. But when Cole fired it up, he only got static. On every channel.

That wasn't right.

Cole popped the canopy and crawled on top of the ex-shuttle, but he found the antenna dish intact and in apparent working order. A quick test even showed power and normal response.

That old pre-combat flutter started deep in Cole's gut,

tightened his balls, made his neck feel exposed and cold. The system check was clean. If Cole could get no signal, someone was jamming them.

Cole slid down the hull and into the cockpit. Jamming meant attack was imminent. He locked the canopy behind him, then stopped. If this was an attack, the Sarkaanans would cut through the locals without effort. Cole couldn't bring himself to hide in his bar and leave the sheep for the wolves.

Cole grabbed his hard beam rifle from behind the bar, double-checked its charge, and ran for the landing field. Three of the traveler ships had already left but four still had their landing gear down and showed no signs of running. Not that they had any visible weapons either. They couldn't without Earth Corps stopping them for every little infraction. Cole ran in front of cockpits, waving his arms and shouting, until each ship had someone willing to come talk to him. Four hard looking, dirty, spacer types. Well, three, plus the scarred kid from earlier.

"We're being jammed," said Cole.

"Snake-heads coming. We know," said a woman with short-cropped black hair and engine grease on her face. "Lookin' for a ride out?"

"I'm looking for help. You use our field, drink in my bar, sell to the locals. Well now we need you."

They laughed. Well, the kid didn't laugh, but he did look down and shake his head. They all headed back for their ships, the kid a little slower than the others.

Wolves, thought Cole. *Nothing but a bunch of lousy wolves when I need sheepdogs.*

There's just me.

Something cold and fatalistic settled into Cole then. The enemy was coming and he was the only one who could do anything about it, the only gun between the locals and the enemy. But he couldn't face them, not in civvies.

If Cole was going to his death, he needed a uniform.

———

COLE DOUBLE-TIMED IT BACK TO HIS COCKPIT, WHERE THE only pieces of old uniform he could find were his garrison cap and combat boots. *Not enough.* Cole dug through his trunks until he found his ancestral kilt, the Douglas family tartan, black-and-gray version. He donned the kilt, boots and cap, picked up his hard beam rifle, and went out to face the enemy.

The night sky of Ganymede glowed with reflections from nearby Io, Europa and Jupiter, more like Earth twilight than the night sky Cole's ancestors knew. Based on the afternoon entry flare, if the Sarkaanans approached, they did so from the north, past the foothills. But Cole jogged these foothills every day, had done so for five years. No one knew them better than he did.

Cole ran for two minutes to the east before turning north, sticking to a secondary ridge to hide his silhouette from the night sky.

Ten minutes out he saw and heard nothing.

Twenty minutes out still nothing.

Thirty minutes out he smelled Sarkaanan.

Cole's last tour included six months on the Sarkaanan front and remembered well their dried shrimp and ammonia scent. Cole closed his eyes to listen harder, and could just make out sibilant tones and what sounded like their language. He dropped to the scrub grass, its harsh texture scratching up his knees and calves as he belly crawled toward the sound.

Cole crested the rise of the nearest high top and there they were tucked into a pocket between hills: four Sarkaanans, a ship, and a land-based antenna pack that Cole figured was the source of the jamming. The ship was a ten-meter-long dull orange tube in the shape of a lazy 's', tapering at the front and back. The aliens themselves looked like upright monitor lizards two meters tall (plus another meter of tail), packing those long rifles his last platoon had dubbed 'Martini-Smiths' because the firing end looked like a martini glass and no one wanted to make enough 's' sounds to pronounce the real name.

But these Sarkaanans wore no uniforms. They dressed in standard spacer clothes of pale green and dark green, nothing like their official burnt orange garb.

That made Cole realize he had already trained his hard beam rifle on the biggest one. He pulled his finger off the trigger. What if they were travelers? Ganymede was a place for travelers. Maybe they didn't mean any harm at all. Maybe they were armed because they expected a hostile welcome...

One of them held up a small remote device. The other three looked at the device, then back at the ship. The leader – or at least Cole assumed the one with the remote was the leader – pushed a button, and Cole saw dim flashes along the ship, followed by sounds like pillows slamming against the floor, followed by hints of concussion, just enough to feel like puffs of air on Cole's face. When the show finished, the ship had collapsed in on itself.

The Sarkaanans had blown their ship. This was a one-way trip for them. Not travelers then. Uniforms or no, they were here to commit an act of war.

What Cole wouldn't have given for a grenade.

Before he even fell flat to the ground, Cole shot the

leader, a flare of pale green and a scent of ozone before the hard beam burned a hole through the enemy's chest. One down.

The other three dove for cover, slithering toward big rocks with a speed and grace that would have made their ancestors proud. Cole got off another shot, but it went wide right.

Cole did some rolling himself, tucking his rifle flat to his chest and trying to move far enough left that they might not be able to meaningfully return fire. At least not yet.

He stopped after about five meters and took a moment to re-orient himself. No immediate sighting of the enemy, but fewer than a half-dozen rocks big enough to hide behind. No sign of returned fire yet either, which meant they knew or guessed that Cole had moved and were waiting to see his next muzzle flash.

Seconds ticked by. Cole had high ground, but they had superior numbers and superior cover. If he let them wait him out, the morning light would make him an easy target.

Speaking of easy targets...

Cole pulled the trigger and burned a hole in the jammer, silencing a deep background hum he hadn't realized he'd heard. Immediately he heard the response puffs from the Martini-Smiths. One ball went wide left, but another shattered less than a meter away, splashing acid that hit Cole's face.

Cole bit through part of his cheek trying not to scream as he squeezed his eyes tight closed and wiped his cheek on a mossy patch of scrub. Pain burned through nerve endings he didn't know he had, tears streaming down his face as he rolled back down a few turns to wipe his face again, on rougher scrub this time.

Breaths fast and shallow, spitting out blood, Cole finally

risked touching his cheek – more fire. His fingers came away bloody, but his fingers didn't burn. He'd cleared the acid.

Cole spat more blood and blinked his eyes to clear the tears, but he knew he wasn't ready. If he went back up there before he got his breathing under control, he'd shake or jump at the wrong time and they'd take him down. He lay where he was and forced himself to count breaths: in two three four, hold one two, out two three four, hold one two. Then again. Then again. And over and over until he felt ready.

He uttered a quick prayer that the governor was smart enough to notice the jamming and put in a distress call the moment the frequencies cleared. Cole might have help come in from the outpost on Europa.

If Europa hadn't been hit.

Cole had to assume he was on his own.

One more deep breath and Cole did a crouch run two dozen paces back to his right before crawling back to his vantage point. No movement.

No.

Wait.

They were slithering again, two of them moving slowly up the hillside, barely visible in the dim light.

Cole fried the first one, but the second whipped its Martini-Smith around and fired faster than Cole expected. The shot fell short, spraying acid in a circle that ended centimeters from Cole's nose. Cole gritted his teeth, trying not to jump, trying not to panic and run from the burning acid. The shot had been reflex. The Sarkaanan hadn't had the angle necessary to have seen Cole's muzzle flash, at least as more than a suggestion.

Dumb luck that the shot almost killed him anyway, and come close enough to make Cole freeze instead of firing the shot that would have kept the snake-head from reaching cover behind a rock. Cole just had to hold his ground. Two were down.

Wait. Two were down and one there behind the rock. Where was the fourth?

The stench of dried shrimp and ammonia hit Cole's nostrils as the fourth Sarkaanan hissed a war cry and leaped to attack, claws ready and ridged mouth wide to bite. Cole swung his hard beam rifle around, but the Sarkaanan knocked it out of his grip with its tail.

Then the Snake-head landed, some hundred and thirty kilos of angry muscle digging claws into Cole's shoulders and mouth coming down at his throat. Pain screamed through Cole's shoulders, but the cry that came out his mouth was at least half fury.

Cole slammed his forehead into the snake-head's jaw, spoiling its strike and making it shake its head, a gesture that, from a human, might have indicated that it was dazed. Cole wasn't sure about that, but he slammed his boots into whatever portion of its anatomy he could reach. It was enough to knock the Sarkaanan off of him, though it raked its claws across Cole's torso, tearing his kilt and carving red gashes as it fell.

Cole's entire existence was pain and blood. Even his vision began to go red and a lightheaded feeling tried to settle in, to tell him to lay down and go to sleep. But Cole kept pushing, forced his arm to go for the *skean dubh* in his boot.

The Sarkaanan leapt mouth first, going for Cole's exposed belly. Cole's shoulder gave out, wouldn't pull, but he managed by an act of will alone to clench his bicep, whipping his boot knife into the throat of the Sarkaanan. Cold blood gushed over Cole, mixing with his own, then some hundred and thirty kilos of snake-head, now dead weight, landed on him.

One more, thought Cole. *Just one more.*

Cole wriggled out from under that body without his arms helping. He couldn't feel his fingers now, and the blood coming out of his shoulders looked darker than it was supposed to. Or maybe the whole world looked a little darker that it was supposed to. And it rang, too, a high-pitched whine in both Cole's ears.

But none of that mattered. One more Sarkaanan was incoming, slithering closer. Cole couldn't see it yet, but he felt it. It had to be taking the cautious approach until given the all-clear. That's how Cole would have handled it.

On the ground next to Cole was his hard beam rifle. His FMA 387 Hard Beam Rifle. 'The best tools for the best men,' the slogan said. But Cole didn't feel like the best man right now. He felt pain, but muffled, like it was on the other side of a mattress, and that wasn't right either.

Focus. Misson.

That was right. One more snake-head incoming, and Cole's weapon was on the ground next to him. But his shoulders didn't want to move, didn't want to pick up the rifle. Not good enough. Cole rolled onto his side and swung his arm over, making his hand land on the rifle. The snake-head had to be getting close. With deliberation, Cole made every numb finger close on the muzzle, then twisted his body to pull his arm and bring the rifle closer.

One little movement at a time. Pick up that rifle, mister! No one dies on your watch!

Then the rifle was in Cole's hands, held up as though presenting arms on a parade ground, though the arms shook too much for good form and the grip looked bloodless.

Cole heard the scrub grass crunch to his left, smelled the dried shrimp and ammonia. No thought, no looking. He just did his best to swing the rifle left and ordered the finger he couldn't feel to pull the trigger over and over, letting off as many hard beams as he could before the world went black.

But then it went black.

AMMONIA SMELL WOKE COLE, AND THE RED INSIDE OF HIS eyelids told him there'd be light when he opened his eyes. His whole body felt strapped in like he'd been taken prisoner. He could hear movement, but no voices yet. He sniffed deep but only got the ammonia. No dried shrimp.

Cole opened his eyes and saw the soul lifting sight of the inside of a triage boat, a battlefield shuttlecraft. The movement was a medic laying out fresh bandages, a woman old enough to have twenty-five years of service herself.

"Hey, you're awake," said the medic with a smile so bright Cole felt a little better already. Or maybe it was the numbness through most of his body. She continued, "Glad you could join us, Captain Douglas."

"Glad ... to be here." Why did he sound so weak? He hated sounding weak. Then it came back to him, the acid, the fight... "Status?"

"You'll live, Captain. Though you're going to need a little help tending bar. Hell of a job back there. You took down a Sarkaanan infiltration team single-handed. That must've--"

"Who ... called you?"

"He did." The medic pointed to the doorway, where the kid with the scar stood, lingering near the hatch like they might recruit him if he took two steps inside. "Refused to leave your side until you woke up."

Cole started to ask a question, but the kid spoke first, with an almost embarrassed shrug. "If I let you get killed I risk the next barkeep not stocking the good whiskey."

Cole tried to laugh, but couldn't manage more than a smile. "You can have a bottle on the house."

BLACK PHANTOM,
GRAY OP

Staring down the barrel of a hard beam pistol. Not how Aren Vestergaard wanted to start the first day of his new life.

Aren gave the Terran Navy a decade, flying black ops missions into Ik-choka and Kwa-Rekk space. Deceptive strikes designed to keep the great alien empires at war with each other. Focus their attention away from the few dozen worlds humans had managed to settle.

Good for the species. Bad for the conscience.

Aren finally had enough. Mustered out last week. That part of his life was over. Time to start anew.

He blew most of his money on a ship of his own and, with the little he had left, set up shop the only place he could afford: New Pretoria, on Io. Lots of space traffic for a new charter pilot, and low rents out here by the spaceport.

And conveniently distant from the family Aren "dishonored" by mustering out. By not living his whole life in the service, as Vestergaards had done for generations.

His family might have changed their tune if they'd known exactly what kind of missions he'd flown. If he'd been allowed to talk about any of it.

But that was forbidden. The risk was too great.

Then again, might not have mattered if they knew. Not with that jingoistic bunch.

Aren rented a little office in a prefab on the edge of the spaceport, away from the big orange buildings with their stylish curves and rows of transplanted madrone trees surrounding open-air landing bays.

Away from anything like style, too.

No terraformed grass or bushes here. Just a skinny, leafless tree out front, and flat yellow dirt surrounding a place so cheap the owner didn't even paint the Quickmesh. It still had the default grayish-white color of an alloy blended from metals only mined here on Io. A little two-story box, with one set of stairs and a tiny space Aren could call his own.

It wasn't much, but it was Aren's.

At least, it was supposed to be.

Aren showed up early that first morning, while the rising sun turned the eastern mountains umber. Excited at the prospect of flying people around without anyone dying. Wore his first civilian clothes in ten years – pale blue stretch fabric shirt that brought out his eyes but would keep him warm through the cool fall day. Relaxed-fit pants, spacer black with lots of pockets. A New Pretoria Afterburners baseball cap over his buzzed blond hair. Shiny new black calf-high boots too, because wearing regular shoes just didn't feel right anymore.

No sidearm. It was a nice change.

Even treated himself to real Terran coffee – rich and smooth – with his breakfast of FakeEggs and the tough salty strips of something that was supposed to be bacon.

He could still taste the coffee lingering over the grease on his tongue as he clanged up the stairs and down the short hallway. Two-Dee was way at the back, of course, but Aren didn't mind. The Quickmesh was enough like ship metal that the tight hallway felt like home. Even smelled kind of like a starship, metallic with a hint of oil. A comforting aroma.

Aren thumbed his key design into the lockpad and the Quickmesh door slid open.

The business end of a hard beam pistol greeted him.

Holding the pistol was an Ik-choka. Like a sapient raccoon, standing upright and more than seven feet tall. Russet fur with lighter blends in patterns. Scattergun rifle strapped to ... his back. Yes. His. It had that little extra broadness through the torso that the male Ik-choka all had.

Twin bandoliers, one of ammo and the other of overstuffed pouches.

All of that Aren noticed before his eyes blinked at the gun.

"I beg your pardon," he said, hands raising to show he had no weapon. "I appear to have the wrong office. If you'll just excuse me—"

"Inside," the Ik-choka said, then chittered something more in his own language. A complaint about waiting if Aren heard it right. The big creature moved his bulk aside with more grace than was fair. Something that big should have been awkward.

Aren stepped into the room. The door slid closed behind him.

The office *looked* like the one Aren was supposed to have. Single room, eight feet both ways. Swing out two-drawer Quickmesh desk with attached chair. Two heavy plastic stools on rollers for clients. Enough fold-out hooks for three jackets. Door in the back for the head. Central light panel in the ceiling.

No windows, of course. Windows were extra.

"Look," said Aren, trying to keep his voice reasonable, "obviously there's been some mistake—"

"Sit." The Ik-choka indicated the desk with the pistol. The creature looked even bigger in the tight space.

As Aren swung out the desk he thought about what he knew. An Ik-choka, wielding a hard beam pistol. A Graven Series Three, to be precise. Military grade. Human make, from Earth itself. Looked well-used.

The weapon was almost as odd as an Ik-choka using a hard beam pistol at all. Every member of the species Aren had ever seen preferred their needle-firing scatterguns. Or lasers.

Aren turned, with the desk behind him, cutting off almost half the room. He looked the Ik-choka in those beady black eyes.

"If you're going to kill me, get it over with. I won't beg."

"Heard that about you." The Ik-choka twitched his whiskers. "Heard some other things too. Now sit."

"I don't take orders anymore. Use that thing or put it away."

The Ik-choka blinked.

Aren grabbed the gun paw with one hand and twisted. Brought his elbow in fast enough to break the furry wrist.

With a squealing chitter it slammed into him. Must have been three hundred pounds of Ik-choka ramming Aren into the metal wall. Crunched most of his body. He tucked his head before impact and still got a mouthful of loose, musky fur.

Aren bit hard. Tasted grit and fur. Yanked at the pistol with both hands.

The Ik-choka squealed again. Tried to pull away.

Aren clamped down with his teeth. Ripped the pistol free. It clattered away.

The Ik-choka slammed a punch into Aren's ribs. Aren gasped pain.

The Ik-choka pulled back, emptying Aren's mouth. Came in for another body slam.

Aren spun with the pressing weight of fur. Swept a leg and sent the big thing belly first into the desk.

Aren opened the door for a fast escape.

And found the barrel of a scattergun rifle waiting for him.

Not much more than a minute later, Aren was seated at his desk, eyeing his two assailants. The Ik-choka chittered soft swear words and wrapped its wrist with firmtape.

Field medicine. Probably criminals then, not civilians looking for payback.

No reason for a human to get payback anyway. And the Ik-choka's partner was human.

A woman. Skin and features the nondescript dark beige of a well-blended heritage. Maybe Aren's age, but not much more. She wore a loose gray spacer jumpsuit, showing as much disdain for fashion as just about humanly possible. Her brown hair was buzzed down as tight as Aren's, and she'd never sought proper treatment for a jagged pink-and-white scar running from her chin to her left ear.

More field medicine?

She kept the scattergun rifle trained on Aren with enviable steadiness. She had a hard beam pistol at her hip too.

Aren kept his hands flat on the desk. The Ik-choka's hard beam pistol was on the floor behind him, but there was no way he could grab it. Not without getting perforated a thousand times before his fingers found the trigger.

Just as well. He didn't want to kill anyone. Not if he didn't have to.

"So," said Aren, "are you going to tell me what this is about or am I going to kick your ass too?"

"Try it."

First words she'd spoken. Her voice was as rough as her scar.

"You guys are the ones with the weapons. I just came here in case any clients showed up. Speaking of..." Aren smiled. "You guys *will* be good enough to fuck off if a paying client shows up, right? I mean, I've got to eat too."

The Ik-choka started to say something, but the woman

cut him off. And she did it in a way Aren had never heard of before.

She chittered like an Ik-choka.

Aren understood a little of their language. Enough to catch that she was talking about someone who wasn't present. He might have understood more but he was too shocked.

Aren hadn't even known a human could *make* those sounds.

The Ik-choka gave a stiff nod, rolling his wrist just past the firm tape and flexing the fingers of his paw. Still looked too comfortable for Aren's liking. After all the effort of breaking the wrist, he wanted the damage to last at least as long as the bruises to his hip, back, and rib cage.

That body slam hurt. And the punch was no treat either.

"You're Aren Vestergaard," she said in English. "You flew for the Navy."

"Those days are done."

"But you've flown into Ik-choka and Kwa-Rekk space. Many times."

Aren said nothing.

"If I think I'm talking to a hologram, I might pull the trigger to check."

"Do it then," said Aren. "None of your business what I did—"

The Ik-choka laughed. A hissing sound that sent shivers down Aren's back. He'd only heard that sound a half-dozen times in his life, and none of them ended well.

It chittered. Aren caught something about falling leaves.

The woman chuckled, a harsh sound, like bad things usually followed that too.

"You understand that?" she said, eyes narrowed.

Aren shook his head.

"My partner here thinks you're afraid we'll kill you over what you've done. That's not true. We'll kill you if you don't do what we want."

"Look ... should I just call you Scar and Smelly or do I get to know the names of my kidnappers?"

"Scar and Smelly will do just fine."

Aren sighed. "Fine then. Scar. You want a flight someplace? I can fly anywhere allowed by law. But you gotta pay me or we won't have any fuel. You know. Fly-fly juice?"

"You bought your ship last week from the shipping yard at Kingston on Mars. Full cells when you picked it up. The only place you've flown is here."

"How do you—"

She smiled. It didn't reach her brown eyes.

"So this is what's going to happen. Your ship is going with us on a little trip into Kwa-Rekk space and back. We'd prefer to do that with you at the helm, alive and intact, but if we have to manage without you—"

"Did you know that every pilot in the Terran Navy learns how to lock controls so no one else can unlock them?"

"Nice try." The scattergun never wavered.

Aren sighed. "So you want me to fly you *unnoticed* somewhere in Kwa-Rekk space? What makes you think—"

"I know what unit you were with."

The words came out fast. Angry. The first sign of emotion in the woman. He could almost believe she did know. Almost.

"No, you—"

"You flew for the Black Phantoms."

All the blood fled from Aren's face, and the air felt ten degrees colder. He didn't dare blink. Black Phantoms was the insider nickname for Unit Seventeen.

A nickname that didn't exist for a unit that didn't exist.

She didn't even name the stalking horse unit, the Gray Ghosts.

No one who knew the name Black Phantoms should have ever spoken it in front of anyone not on active duty. Least of all in front of an alien.

"That's right," Scar said. "Deny it all you like. But you know what I said and you know what it means. Now, are you—"

"Yes." Aren nodded. "I'll fly you there and back."

Aren needed to know more about these two. Maybe she was a retiree he'd never heard of. Maybe she'd saved the Ik-choka's life, or it hated its own species. Something like that.

Or maybe Aren would have to kill them after all. Damn it.

WHEN THE T-DRIVE PINGED AND THE STARS TWISTED BACK TO their proper positions, Aren's ship the *Freedom* slipped back into normal space in the sensor shadow of a burnt out moon above a planet that Aren's star charts designated Pi Epsilon Six.

Aren knew the name for it in the Sarkaanan language of the Kwa-Rekk Federation, but he could never have pronounced it. Too much hissing.

The star in this system was smaller and paler than Earth's sun, but Pi Epsilon Six orbited closer to that star than Earth to its sun. A hot planet, with lush jungles near the equator where most of the life was concentrated in the Sarkaanan equivalent of cities.

Dry deserts and tundra filled most of the three huge continents. Smaller oceans than Earth, none reaching the magnetic poles.

Aren liked to pretend that the *Freedom* wasn't cobbled together from cast-off Navy parts, but the shape of it made the truth clear to even a casual observer. And Aren, he could tell what kind of ship each section came from. Round bridge salvaged from a medium freighter, with a big concave viewing screen in front of the pilot's station. Narrow wings from a troop transport, sticking straight out from the frame, but with that stylish little bend toward the tips. Wide body also from a troop transport, converted for civilian passenger comfort.

Most obviously a round cargo pod in the back above the engine. That just screamed Naval shipyard. Damn thing might as well have weapons on it.

The ship was a mutt, but it would hold together until Aren could afford a new one. Or even a good used ship.

Someday. Assuming he survived this little jaunt.

Probably never then.

Aren was back in the pilot seat when the T-drive pinged. Displays overlaid the viewing screen, with star chart data, planetary readings, sensor locations on the six nearest fighters on patrol. All narrow, snake-like designs of the Kwa-Rekk military.

Two packs of three. One pack off toward the horizon, heading for the far side of the planet. One pack moving closer.

No more than two minutes before the moon's shadow stopped giving him cover.

Smelly loomed behind Aren again, scattergun rifle tip pressed to the back of his neck. Scar said it was in case Aren had any ideas about betraying them, but Aren thought it was payback for the wrist.

No way they knew about his hidden compartment.

At least Smelly had to hunch in the bridge or hit his

head every time he moved. Still, his musky scent was going to linger. If Aren got out of this alive, his bridge wouldn't smell right for weeks.

"What are you going to do about those fighters?" Scar leaned over the controls to point at the approaching markers on the screen.

"Back off and I'll tell you," said Aren. When he no longer felt like someone was waiting to smother him with a hot, furry blanket, Aren spun around in his seat.

The bridge was the size of his office, if someone had shaved the corners round. More gray than white, and he'd had the other seats pulled out when he had the other control panels turned into metal counters. Aren was his only crew, so why not route all controls through the pilot station?

This didn't leave Scar and Smelly much room to maneuver in the tight space, but they certainly had the exit blocked.

"Well?" said Scar.

"I intend to let them catch us." Aren shrugged. "They'll probably kill us but—"

Smelly chittered something too fast for Aren to follow and raised his scattergun.

"You pull that trigger and you'll blast every control on the bridge. Good luck then."

Scar nodded and Smelly lowered the rifle.

"We need to tell him," she said.

Smelly started to protest, then turned and left the bridge.

"Tell me what?" Aren said, folding his arms. "Better say it quick, 'cause in about ninety seconds—"

"My name is Paula Renault." She nodded toward the bridge door. "He's Ke-Aka. His mate's down there. Captured during a raid about a month ago, when the snake heads hit her city. Officially she's dead. The Ik-Choka don't care because she doesn't know anything that can hurt their military. Or at least, nothing worth a rescue attempt."

Aren got a sinking feeling in his gut.

"Raid on Gamma Twelve?"

Renault nodded. From the look in her eye, Aren didn't need to tell her why he asked. Gamma Twelve had been a noisy and public response to his last mission against the Kwa-Rekk Federation. Nasty piece of work that implicated the Ik-choka, of course.

Aren hadn't given the orders. Hadn't even placed the explosives. Hadn't done any groundwork at all on that mission. But he'd flown it. He was responsible...

Aren lowered his head in shame.

Then spun around in his chair.

Twenty seconds and closing.

Aren keyed the thrusters.

"What are you doing?" Renault cried. "They'll—"

"Not a good time to distract me," Aren sang.

Aren matched the pack's speed, holding tight to the moon's shadow. Followed the curve of the husk while the Sarkaanan pilots followed the curve of the planet.

Ninety seconds later Aren was clear. He was feeling positively clever until he spotted something at the edge of his sensor range.

A third pack. Coming in fast now.

No way he could get the *Freedom* down to the planet. Not without alerting the locals.

"Can you handle a drop?" said Aren, popping open his hidden compartment and grabbing his laser pistol and holster. He strapped them to his belt. "Can Ke-Aka?"

"*From here?*"

"Yep." Keyed a quick program into the computer. "Come on."

Then he was past Renault and down the corridor. Ke-Aka was hunching in the center of the passenger common area cleaning his scattergun. Right there in the middle of the affixed round plastic tables and chairs. Not even spreading out on the padded bench seats around the perimeter or in front of the big, starboard hatch doors.

"Assemble it fast," said Aren, running for one of those bench seats. "We're jumping."

Ke-Aka started to chitter, then said, "W-what about the ship?"

"I know how to hide a ship in a lunar shadow. You'll have to trust me."

"What about those fighters?" said Renault.

"You wanted a Black Phantom?" Aren got in her face and stared down those brown eyes. "This is how it works. Follow my lead or call this off."

Renault nodded.

Aren dove back to the bench seats along the port side. Opened a panel along the bottom and pulled jumpers out of a crate. The one thing Aren stole when he mustered out. He'd be damned if he gave up anything that useful.

He tossed one of the strapped, fist-sized black pods to each of Renault and Ke-Aka and took one for himself and tucked another into one of the pockets in his pants.

Following the humans' lead, Ke-Aka slipped his big, furry arms through the straps. Too tight on the big Ik-Choka, but Aren couldn't help that.

"They're made for humans, I'm afraid." Aren adjusted the straps for Ke-Aka, then stepped up to the starboard hatch doors. "But we have humans that grow to your height.

Or near enough. So I'm hoping this will work. It's our only shot though."

When Renault and Ke-Aka joined him at the hatch, he said, "Smack 'em!"

He reached over his shoulder and smacked the pod on his back, while Renault did her own and then Ke-Aka's.

Each was surrounded by a tight protective field as wings with hand grips popped out behind them and a tiny engine hummed to life. Aren opened the hatch.

He jumped into space, and the other two followed.

***

THIS WAS FLYING.

No ship. No sensors. Just speeding through space.

Swift. Smooth. Effortless.

Couldn't see the fighters from here, but they couldn't see Aren either. Jumpers were some of the finest tech humans had ever produced. Made the Black Phantoms possible in the first place.

A swift way into and out of almost anywhere. Invisible to sensors. So far, anyway.

They crossed the black in almost no time. Then down, down through the outer layers of the atmosphere and dropping. Renault tried to get Aren's attention. Probably wanted to talk about where they were going.

Jumpers had no comm system.

Didn't matter. Sarkaanan settlement layouts were the same all over the Kwa-Rekk Federation. They built in clutches, civilian population toward the center and military surrounding in a thin shell.

Prisons were always way off to one side. Isolated. They'd

be up in the dry area. The tundra. The *Freedom's* sensors had picked up two settlements in the tundra. One big, one small.

Aren was betting the small settlement was where Ke-Aka's mate was being held. A gut call, but Aren's gut had proven itself over the years.

They set down among some low foothills. Scrub grass and high wind. Tiny bushes with purple berries.

Cold. Too cold. Aren was shivering the moment he de-activated his jumper. Should've thought to grab a jacket.

Aren turned to the others and Ke-Aka lifted him with one paw. The other paw held that hard beam pistol again, trained on Aren's face.

"What the—"

Ke-Aka was chittering again, too fast for Aren.

"Ke-Aka wants to know how you knew *right* where his mate is being held."

"Put me down. Now."

"It took us a week to find out where. And that was after we knew what planet."

Aren stared straight into those angry black eyes.

"Last chance."

Renault touched Ke-Aka's shoulder and the big Ik-choka twitched his whiskers. He set Aren back on the scrub grass, and lowered the pistol but didn't put it away.

Aren's anger boiled over. He spat out words in a tone he thought he'd left behind.

"No more," said Aren. "No more threats. No more guns pointed at me. No more. Do it one more time and I'll kill you both and go home. If you think I can't, then you don't know what the Black Phantoms are after all."

"How-w did you know-w?" asked Ke-Aka.

"The only thing more predictable than a Sarkannan settlement is an Ik-choka's temper. Now." Aren shifted his glare from Ik-choka to human and back. "Do we understand each other?"

They nodded.

"Good. Do you two know which cell she's in? Or do I have to figure out everything myself?"

"Third circle, cell ninety," said Renault. "But I saw a facility on Tau Delta that—"

"That's mostly a human settlement. The snake heads build differently among themselves." Aren rubbed at his chin and looked off the direction of the prison. He could just make out the sloping shape of the main building. "I hope you two were smart enough to bring some explosives."

Ke-Aka patted a few of those overstuffed bandolier pouches.

"Good," said Aren. "Then I know just what to do."

THE CENTRAL BUILDING OF THE PRISON WAS BUILT FROM A single tube of bright red metal. The tube itself was ten feet in diameter, looping first around in a circle, then up on top of itself in shrinking circles. The loops ended in a single observation dome at the top, with a turret. Long single panel of one-way window like a black racing stripe the whole way up.

Common design for a Sarkaanan building. The red marked it as prison administration. Inside the gap created by the spiral would be a second building, egg-shaped, that held up to four of the most dangerous prisoners.

That Ke-Aka's mate was in a circle meant she was in one of the underground cells surrounding the administration building. Easier to get to, but exposed to attack from pretty much any direction. Especially that turret, but also the guards that roamed in packs of four.

Aren lay on his belly in dry, yellow grass. Still shivering in the cold. Grateful for the baseball cap that held in at least some of his body heat. He could smell the ammonia and dried shrimp odor of the Sarkaanan everywhere, even stronger here than the musky scent of the big Ik-choka who lay prone next to him.

Aren had the scattergun rifle now. Didn't make him feel any better. But then, "feeling better" would have meant a nice, boring day waiting for clients and a lunch of ham-and-cheddar on pressed wheat. Apparently too much to ask in this life.

How much longer would Renault need?

Boom.

Every guard Aren could see ran toward the sound, toward the far side of the main building.

Sarkaanan still looked like their monitor lizard fore-bears, though with smaller tails and articulated mouths. They carried those bell-ended Martini Smith rifles of theirs and wore dark red uniforms that marked them as prison guards.

Aren was on his feet and running before he heard the second explosion. Same area as the first.

Ke-Aka outpaced him, running on all fours.

Chuk chuk chuk sounds now from the turret. And the faint chatter of a scattergun that had to be Renault firing at more guards.

The fourth and final explosion came as Aren passed the fourth circle, visible by rough dirt covering the cell iris ports. Round holes in the scrub grass. Cell ninety meant the cell ninety degrees from the administration building center, with the building start forming the zero line.

Ke-Aka was already strapping the last of their explosives to the cell's lock panel as Aren approached.

"No!" he shouted, cursing himself for the noise. "The middle! The iris port center!"

Didn't these people know anything? Damn fool nearly sealed his mate in a tomb.

A pack of running guards heard his shouts. Turned. Not even fifty yards away.

One of them raised a communicator.

Aren snapped a shot. Drove a needle through the hand holding the comm.

Didn't help. Another let out a scream of battle that was sure to call more guards.

Scattergun chatter in the background. Cold wind picking up.

Aren knelt, spitting instructions at Ke-Aka. Laying down cover fire.

The Sarkaanan guards dove. No good. They crawled faster than some humans could run.

Two were closing. Two more raised their rifles.

First shots were wide. Balls of acid shattering and sizzling the dirt.

Aren held that trigger down. Scattergun shaking his arms. Needles flying into the dirt. Drove back the crawlers. Made the shooters roll aside.

Something tight in Aren's gut. Gripped his lungs. No more dead. Please. No more dead.

Finally he heard the smaller *boom* of the iris port blowing open.

Aren spared a hand to toss Ke-Aka the fourth jumper. Blew his aim. Shots flew wild high.

Pain.

Searing pain. Right thigh. Acid ball.

Aren dove into the grass. Bent a knee and dragged himself to clear the acid. Pain jangled his nerves. Clenched his jaw. His neck.

Aren came up shooting. Wide arc, muzzle low. Drove back the guards he knew about and sent the guards who shot him diving for cover.

Chuk chuk chuk

Huge balls of acid tore up the ground nearby. Splashed Aren's gun arm with more pain.

Aren howled with rage and sprayed the area with needles. Maybe he hit something. Maybe not. Sometimes on sleepless nights, he'd wonder.

"Ready!" said Ke-Aka at last.

Aren threw down the scattergun and slapped the jumper on his back.

Just like that he was airborne, flying low and away. Ke-Aka and a smaller Ik-choka right behind him.

Too fast for the Sarkaanan to hit.

Low they flew until they reached foothills. Only then, certain that they were clear, did they turn back toward space.

***

TURNED OUT RENAULT KNEW A THING OR TWO ABOUT treating acid burns. She had cobbled together her own neutralizer that was almost as good as visiting a hospital. Aren would bear a nasty scar on his thigh and a smaller twin on his arm, but that was all.

He didn't lose a limb, which was the big concern.

Field medicine. Patching soldiers up as long as there'd been soldiers.

Aren had the ship hiding deep inside the husk of the

burnt out moon. The four of them were in the *Freedom's* common area. Aren stretched out on one of the bench seats, the leg of his pants cut away, same with that shirt sleeve. Regular white bandages wrapped around his leg and arm.

Renault kept poking at the area around his leg wound. Checking her handiwork maybe. Then again, maybe not. She had a different look in her eye since they got back, and her touch was gentler.

Ke-Aka and his mate were over in the corner, holding each other and talking in low voices.

"How much longer do we have to stay here?" she said, voice as soft as her touch.

"I've got enough emergency rations to last us a day or two. That should give them time to get over the initial rush of looking for us. Probably assume we'd be gone by now."

"Why aren't we?"

"Drawback of the jumpers. Nowhere near as fast as a ship. In the corps we'd probably have a rendezvous with a ship pulling us out. Short of that, if we'd prepped for this properly, we'd be laying in here for a week."

"Might not be so bad," Renault said with a twitch of her lips.

"You broke into my office and pointed a gun at me. You—"

"I get it," she said, raising her hands in surrender, but not looking away. "Too soon."

Aren couldn't stop himself from chuckling at that. Whoever this Renault woman was, she'd been military or mercenary. No one else had that sense of humor.

"Are you sorry we did this?" she asked.

Aren looked over at Ke-Aka and his mate. Something tight in his gut loosened just a little bit.

"No," he said.

"Good, because—"

"Wait." Aren dragged himself to a sitting position over the protest of most of his body. "How do you know about the Black Phantoms? And me? And—"

"Staff Corporal Davidson."

She was watching Aren's eyes when she said it, and laughed at his grimace. Staff Corporal Davidson was a legend in the Navy. Most people thought he didn't exist. Most of those who knew he was real wished they didn't.

The man was a corporal with more power than an admiral, because he was the center around which supply and logistics operated.

He knew everything and everyone, and he could get anyone anything, anywhere.

"Well if that son of a bitch sent you to me, he better make sure I get paid or I'll be selling this ship when we get back."

Renault settled onto the seat beside him, still smiling.

"He promised that if you did it, he'd make sure you were well paid."

"Why didn't you say so earlier?"

"Would you have taken a regular charter this deep into Kwa-Rekk space?" She didn't need the answer, so she kept talking. "And that's not all. There are others like Ke-Aka. Others with lives ruined by war. Others you could help. *We* could help."

Aren still wasn't sure how far he trusted her. But looking over at Ke-Aka and his mate stirred something inside him.

This could be a new life. A good life.

"Davidson better get me fuel for those jumpers then too. Because we're going to need them."

SIGN UP FOR STEFON'S NEWSLETTER

Stefon loves to keep in touch with his readers, and loves to keep you reading. The best way for him to do both is for you to sign up for his newsletter.

Sign up at http://www.stefonmears.com/join

If you sign up for Stefon's newsletter, you get...

- Monthly updates about his publishing and travel schedules
- His latest news, in brief, and answers to reader questions
- A free short story for signing up
- List-only offers and occasional specials
- Plus a free short story every month!

ABOUT THE AUTHOR

Stefon Mears used to bug his dad for questions about the Navy, so he could apply them to space stories. Stefon has more than thirty books to his credit, and he never stops writing. He earned his M.F.A. in Creative Writing from N.I.L.A., and his B.A. in Religious Studies (double emphasis in Ritual and Mythology) from U.C. Berkeley. He's a lifelong gamer and fantasy fan. Stefon lives in Portland, Oregon, with his wife and three cats.

Look for Stefon online:
www.stefonmears.com
himself@stefonmears.com